Kim Rentola

Kim Rentola

The Wind in the Willows

Adapted from Kenneth Grahame's classic storybook
Retold by Desmond Marwood

Brown Watson
ENGLAND

CONTENTS

The Riverbank

Mole had never seen a river before. So, when he met Water Rat, he was excited to learn all about life on the water and those who lived on the riverbanks.

Rat showed Mole around his riverside home. It was built into the riverbank, just above the water level. Rat's little blue rowing boat was tied up to the landing stage, just outside the front door.

It was so warm and sunny, that the new friends decided to spend the day exploring the river.

Rat packed a picnic hamper full of nice things to eat and drink. "I'll be able to show you so many things to do with our life on the river," he told Mole, as he helped him into the boat.

They floated gently down the river. From time to time, Rat stopped rowing to point out special things to Mole. It was a great big exciting new world for Mole. In the water he could see fishes swimming beneath the boat. He had never ever seen fishes! On the riverbanks were all sorts of small creatures and birds.

Many of them were so different from those he had met in the grassy fields above his own home, which was beneath the ground.

"What's that place?" asked Mole, pointing to a dark and dismal woodland, with huge branches reaching out over the water's edge.

"Ah! That's the Wild Wood," Rat told him. "We don't go in there unless we really have to and I'd advise you to keep away also. Most of those who live there are not very friendly, especially to strangers."

The two friends found a good place for their picnic and Rat rowed the boat towards the riverbank.

No sooner were they settled down and set to eat, than Otter popped out of the water and onto the riverbank beside them.

Then came a rustle from the bushes and Badger appeared. Being a very polite fellow, he turned immediately and disappeared. He said he was sorry to have barged in. He didn't know Ratty had visitors, or "company" as he called them.

Rat asked Otter who else he'd
seen on the river that day.
"Only old Toad rowing along in
his boat," replied Otter. "Or, I
should say, *trying* to row," he
added and they both laughed.
They knew that mucking
about in boats was the latest
thing Toad had started to do.
"Toad's always got a new craze
to do something or other," Rat
told Mole, who hadn't heard
anything about the famous
Mr.Toad until that moment.

"The last craze he had was to
live on a houseboat. That didn't last long. Dear old Toad
soon missed the comfort of his own home," added Rat.
"Does Toad live on the riverbank?" asked Mole.
"Oh, yes," Rat told Mole, "but *his* riverside home is a little
bit posher than *my* riverside home. Toad's home is called
Toad Hall and it is one of the best houses in the district.
I'll take you there, one day."

Just then, Toad came into sight, moving along the river in his rowing boat. The oars waggled all over the place and his feet kicked in the air, as he and his boat wobbled away into the distance.

"Good day!" called out Rat. "What a beautiful day to be out on the river." But Toad was so frantically busy trying to row his boat that he didn't hear him, let alone see Rat waving to him from the riverbank.

"Boats won't be old Toad's craze for very much longer if he can't row better than that!" laughed Rat. "He does like to be able to do things properly, so he can show off to everyone else."

Rat looked round to see Otter had already popped back into the river just as quickly as he'd first popped out.

Rat and Mole finished off their picnic, cleared everything neatly away and set off for home. It was on the way that Mole suddenly wanted to try and row the boat, but Rat didn't think that was such a good idea.

"Hey! Be careful or you'll have us overboard," cried Rat, as Mole tried to grab the oars. Rat tumbled backwards off his seat into the bottom of the boat. Mole could not get hold of the oars properly and he fell forwards on top of Rat and – splash! – over he went into the water.

Rat was a good swimmer. He pulled Mole to the safety of the riverbank. Then, he brought the boat to the riverbank, as well as the oars and the picnic basket, which were all in danger of floating away.

Rat scooped the water out of the boat and made everything tidy for them to continue their journey back home. While he did this, Rat made sure Mole went jogging up and down the riverbank to help him to get dry. Poor old Mole! He was so sorry that he'd started all their troubles in the first place by trying to grab the oars from Rat.

"I don't know what came over me, really I don't," he moaned. "Oh! Please do forgive me!" he pleaded with Rat. Of course, Rat did forgive Mole, but made him promise never to do anything like that again and always to first learn the proper way to do things. "Rowing a boat can be a tricky thing until you know how to do it properly," Rat told Mole. "It's just one of the things you learn how to do if you live on the river." Mole began to feel much happier when Rat promised that one day he would teach him how to row a boat.

When they got back home, Rat made Mole dry out properly in front of a warm fire. They ate a good supper and Rat invited Mole to stay the night so that he could have a good night's sleep after his first very busy day on the river.

Mole was soon fast asleep and dreaming of what had, for him, been a day of great adventure. He had seen so many new things, enjoyed a delicious picnic and had taken his first ever ride in a boat. Also, he had met new friends. Most important though was meeting Water Rat, who would turn out to be his greatest friend of all!

The Open Road

Rat and Mole spent all of the long, hot summer together. Then, one day, Mole told Rat he'd like to meet Mr. Toad. "I've heard so much about him," said Mole, "and I do so want to meet him."

"Certainly!" agreed Rat. "Get the boat out and we'll go up to Toad Hall at once!"

They went round a bend in the river and came upon a very big house with well-kept gardens and lawns reaching down to the water's edge.

"That is Toad Hall," announced Rat, "the home of Mr. Toad! Many have seen it from outside, but Toad only likes his special friends to call on him."

"Toad is quite good natured
even if he does boast a lot. I'm
sure he won't mind us landing here,"
explained Rat. They took a small turning
off the main river and past a sign which read:
"PRIVATE! No Landing Allowed!"
"Toad built this place when boating was the big thing in
his life," Rat told Mole. "I wonder what his latest craze is
now he's fed up with boating?"

Rat rowed his boat past the "PRIVATE!" sign. He and Mole tied up the boat outside the boathouse. It looked as though it could do with cleaning from top to bottom and a good tidying up.

Rat and Mole found Toad resting in a garden chair, with a large map spread out before him. He jumped up to give his visitors a joyful welcome.

"You're the very friends I want!" cried Toad, although he'd never met Mole before. "You've got to help me. It's most important."

Toad told them he'd given up boats some time ago.

"I've discovered what is the greatest excitement of my life," he told them. "Come, let me show you!"

Toad led the way to a yard in front of the coach house.
There, they saw a gypsy caravan, shining with bright
yellow paint and with green and red wheels. A happy
yellow canary sang a sweet tune from its golden cage,
hanging by the caravan door.

Toad was excited. He waved his arms in the direction of
the caravan and cried out to Rat and Mole:

"There you are! Have you got everything we need to
start our journey on the open road this very afternoon."

Rat didn't like the way Toad used words such as *"we"* and
"our" and *"this afternoon"*.

He knew that when Toad said *"we"* he meant all three of them – Toad, Mole and himself. He knew that when Toad said *"our"* journey, he meant *"their"* journey as well! When Toad said *"this afternoon"*, he really meant immediately - right now! He also knew that there was absolutely no way of getting out of it!

Rat was quite right, because before they hardly knew what they were doing, he and Mole had fallen under the spell of Toad's enthusiasm. They rounded up Toad's old grey horse, harnessed it to the caravan and set off rolling along the highway with Toad at the reins.

After a beautiful summer's day amongst the fields and country lanes, the tired travellers spent that night on a common. They sat on the grass and ate supper beneath a starry sky and yellow full moon.

By the second day of their travels, Rat and Mole made sure that Toad did his share of the hard work. They made him help look after the horse, prepare some of the meals and do some of the tidying up. Already, Toad was showing signs that he was not finding caravan life so restful after all. Toad moaned when he had to wash dishes and groaned when he had to fetch water. His poor back was aching and his whole body seemed full of pain. When they set off again, Rat guessed it would not be long before Toad's love of life in a caravan would be over and finished and then he and Mole could go back to their life on the riverbank.

The travellers set off. Mole walked ahead,
talking to the horse. Rat was further back, listening
to more of Toad's boastful tales. Suddenly, they turned
to see a cloud of dust over the road some way behind
them. There was also the sound of: "Poop! Poop! –
Poop! Poop!"
In no time at all, the dust was all around them and they
jumped for safety into the nearest ditch.

"Poop! Poop! – Poop! Poop!" came

the warning sound of the monster's horn.

They all had a quick glimpse of the shiny glass, red leather

and brass fittings of a magnificent motor car. It swept by

at such speed that it soon dwindled away to a speck on the

horizon. The driver, a very smart-looking gentleman, was

still sounding the horn – "Poop! Poop! – Poop! Poop!"

Shocked by all that was happening, the old grey horse reared up and then fell backwards, pushing the caravan into the ditch by the roadside. There was a tremendous crashing noise and the beautiful yellow caravan turned onto its side.

It was a complete wreck!

Mole was sorry their holiday had ended so sadly. Rat wasn't too upset, but Toad was in a sort of daze. Rat and Mole rescued the little bird in its cage and gathered their belongings.

They put the horse in a nearby stable. Then, they bought railway tickets for all three of them, as well as the bird, to take them back to the nearest station to Toad Hall.

Toad would not allow them to report the damage caused by the car to the police. "What?" he cried out. *"Complain about that car – that beautiful, heavenly motor car – never, I say, never!"*

Like the good friends they were, Rat and Mole made sure Toad was returned safely to Toad Hall.

They left him tucked up in bed. Poor Toad – he still looked to be in a daze and all he kept saying was: "Poop! Poop! – Poop! Poop!" Rat knew then that Toad's next craze would be for motor cars!

The Wild Wood

Mole was still sharing Rat's home as summer passed into autumn and winter came along. One day, while Rat dozed in front of the fire, Mole decided to set off by himself to visit Badger at his home in the Wild Wood.

Rat had warned Mole many times about the Wild Wood and its dangers. "Keep away from there!" he always said.

"It can't be all that bad a place," thought Mole. "After all, dear old Badger lives there and he's a really good chap, so I'm told. I'm sure I'll be quite safe." With that, Mole put on his warmest clothes and set off on his journey.

The Wild Wood was dark
and gloomy. The wind whispered strange
noises and creatures Mole could not see were
running all around him. Little beady eyes seemed to be
watching him through the dark bushes and the thick
undergrowth. Mole was starting to feel very afraid. In a
panic, he ran this way and that. He tripped and fell into
a hole at the foot of a beech tree. Trembling with fright
and cold, Mole dug down into a bed of warm leaves.

Back at home, Rat was worried when he woke up to find Mole had gone out on his own. He could see footprints from his front door leading up the bank and on towards the Wild Wood.

Rat put on warm clothes. He knew about the dangers of the Wild Wood and he pushed a pair of pistols into his belt and picked up a heavy walking stick. Then he set off to search for his dear friend Mole.

"I did tell Mole never to go into the Wild Wood on his own," said Rat. "He doesn't know his way around, or some of the nasty folk who live there. I do hope he doesn't come to any harm before I find him."

Inside the Wild Wood, Rat
searched for many hours.
"Where are you, Mole?" he
called, time and time again.
"Don't be afraid – it's old
Ratty – I've come to take
you home!"

Rat called Mole's name again
and again. Each time there was no reply.
"Mole!" Rat called out at the top of his voice. "Can you
hear me, Mole?"

Then, Rat heard a small voice call out: "I'm over here!"

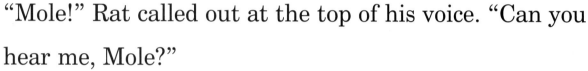

"Over where?" called back Rat. "Here, down a hole at the
bottom of this big tree," replied Mole.

Rat soon found Mole and let himself down into the hole to
see if his friend was safe and sound and hadn't
hurt himself when falling down.

The two friends were happy to be together
again. It was so warm and cosy on the
bed of old leaves at the bottom of the
hole, that they decided to rest there for
a while. They soon fell fast asleep.

By the time Rat and Mole woke up and climbed out of their hole, heavy snow had fallen. Everything in the wood was covered with a thick white blanket. Rat's footprints into the wood were hidden by the snow. He had hoped to follow them to guide them out of the wood. Also, the covering of thick snow made it impossible to recognise any trees or bushes or other landmarks.

Rat and Mole had no idea where they were and had no way of telling. They were completely lost!

Rat walked this way and that. Mole followed and then cried out in pain. He had tripped over what looked like a metal foot-scraper sticking up through the snow and had hurt his leg quite badly.

Mole helped Rat to scoop away more snow from around the footscraper and found a doormat. Soon, they uncovered a door, set back in a mound of snow-covered earth. There was a bell-pull and a brass plate upon which were the words: "Mr.Badger". "Hurrah!" cried Mole. "We've found out where Mr. Badger lives after all. I hope it's not too late to call on him."

Mole jumped up to reach the bell-pull and the bell clanged. Rat banged the door with his stick, calling out: "Badger! Are you at home? Please open up – it's your friend Rat! My friend Mole is with me and he so wants to meet you. What's more, we've lost our way home!"

Rat and Mole heard footsteps from the other side of the door. Then came the sound of chains rattling and locks being turned. Finally, the door opened and a surprised Badger appeared, lighting his way with a candle.

Badger was wearing his dressing gown and old slippers.
Rat guessed he must have been on his way to bed, as by
now it was getting very late in the day.

Badger cleaned the scratches on Mole's leg and covered
them with sticking plaster. He made them both put on
spare dressing gowns and slippers, while their clothes
were hung up to dry.

Badger served them a wonderful supper. Afterwards,
they sat with him in front of the warm kitchen fire. They
told him about their day's adventure, which had begun
with Mole setting out by himself to look for Badger's
home in the Wild Wood.

"Well, it's time we were all in bed," Badger told them. "The weather is bad and it's much too late for you to find your way home now."

Badger insisted they stayed the night and showed them to his spare bedroom. It was really a storeroom for his apples, turnips, potatoes, bags full of nuts and jars of honey.

There was a space, though, for two small beds which Rat and Mole tumbled into and enjoyed a good night's sleep.